The Shoemaker Extraordinaire

by
Steve Light

Harry N. Abrams, Inc.,
Publishers

O nce upon a time there was a man named Hans Crispin, who traveled throughout the land. He was called a "shoemaker extraordinaire" because he could create a shoe that fit each customer just right.

One day Hans Crispin met
a man outside a village.

"I'm Hans Crispin, shoemaker extraordinaire! Would you like a new pair of shoes?"

"Shoes! I have plenty of shoes," replied the short man, "unless you have a pair to make me taller."

"Taller!" answered Hans. "How simple. I have the perfect pair!"

Hans gave him
a pair of shoes
that could only
be made by a
shoemaker
extraordinaire.
The man ran
through the
village, telling
everyone of the
wonderful
shoemaker.

Soon many people came to Hans in search of shoes. A little girl whom everyone overlooked wanted to be the center of attention. With her new shoes, she would never be a wallflower again.

A woman who had many dogs was always tired from walking them. With Hans's new shoes, her dogs wore out before she did!

When a fisherman's boat sprung a leak, he did not need a new one. He had shoes from Hans.

**A man who was tired and had no pep
asked Hans if he could rev him up.**

Everyone in town was
pleased with Hans and
his work extraordinaire,
except for the cobbler.
He was bitter because no
one came to buy his
ordinary shoes anymore.
So he devised a plan to
rid the village of his rival.

The cobbler told Hans that the giant, Barefootus, needed shoes.

"Why doesn't the giant want you to make the shoes for him?" asked Hans.

"Only a shoemaker extraordinaire like yourself could make shoes for a giant," said the cobbler slyly.

Hans wholeheartedly agreed and went off to accomplish his task. He did not realize that the giant was not looking for a new pair of shoes but for dinner instead.

DO NOT ENTER

Danger
Barefootus the
Giant this way

WATCH OUT!

DANGER
Giant
this way

BEWARE
of the
GIANT!

YIKES!

Hans soon found a trail of things stepped on, stumbled over, and bumped into. Following it, he found Barefootus.

"I'm Hans Crispin, shoemaker extraordinaire, ready to make you a pair of shoes," said Hans.

"Shoes? I can't eat shoes, and since I cannot find my garden or my livestock, I will lock you up and eat you for breakfast tomorrow!" grumbled Barefootus.

Realizing the cobbler had tricked
him, Hans ran as fast as he could.
Chasing him, the giant stubbed his toe. This made
him grumble all the more, and he almost ate Hans
right then and there!

That night, locked in a cage, Hans knew he
needed a plan, a plan extraordinaire! So he
set to work.

"Where's my breakfast?"
Barefootus bellowed as he
came in the next morning,
looking for Hans.

"In the garden and in the
barn!" said Hans. "These shoes
will help you find them!"

"I said, I need no shoes!"
shouted Barefootus.

"But these are shoes extraordinaire!" beamed Hans. Barefootus slipped them on and could finally see the world at his feet. Instead of being breakfast, Hans shared in Barefootus's morning meal. The giant and Hans became fast friends, and decided to teach the cobbler a lesson.

The next day they journeyed to the
village, straight to the cobbler's shop.
   "Where is the cobbler?" the giant
roared while Hans hid. "I have eaten
one shoemaker today and enjoyed the
taste, so I came here to eat another!"
   The cobbler, at hearing this, ran
away and was never heard from again.

The Giant Shoe Shop

"Is the giant going to eat us?" asked the villagers.

"No, this is my friend Barefootus," replied Hans. And he told the villagers what had happened.

"Any friend of yours is a friend of ours," they said. So Barefootus decided to stay in town and learn the cobbler's trade as the villagers now had need of one.

For Hans soon decided his work there was done and it was time to move on. Saying good-bye to all his new friends, Hans went looking for new towns and new people—people who would need shoes extraordinaire!

Author's Note

One day in the classroom a wonderful thing happened. While my students were painting on large paper taped to the floor, some drips and small spills were accidently stepped in and tracked across the floor and our paintings. The children noticed the interesting patterns that each shoe print left behind. I was working on the Shoemaker story at the time and became fascinated with the bottoms of shoes and how they could be inked and printed to make spectacular patterns. That is how the hand-printed papers were made, all using the soles of shoes. I searched used clothing shops, cobbler shops, toy stores, and even asked my students for old shoes. After printing the papers, I cut and collaged them into the pictures you see on these pages.

The main character's name, Hans Crispin, is derived from Saint Crispin, the patron saint of European cobblers, who made shoes for the poor at night from leather supplied by an angel. His first name is in homage to Hans Christian Andersen, the beloved storyteller.

Patterns and colors are all around us—my hope is to draw children into this world and show them that spilled and stepped-in paint can make beautiful art, and that their shoes can carry them anywhere their imagination can think of.

Designer: Becky Terhune
Production Manager: Hope Koturo

Library of Congress Cataloging-in-Publication Data

Light, Steven.
The shoemaker extraordinaire / by Steven Light.
p. cm.
Summary: Hans Crispin is such a creative shoemaker that he manages to befriend a hungry giant, and together they scare off the village cobbler who tried to trick Hans.
ISBN 0-8109-4236-4
[1. Fairy tales. 2. Shoemakers—Fiction. 3. Shoes—Fiction. 4. Giants—Fiction.]
I. Title.
PZ8.L53Sh 2003
[E]—dc21

2002009803

Published in 2003 by Harry N. Abrams, Incorporated, New York
All rights reserved. No part of the contents of this book may be reproduced without the written permission of the publisher.

Printed and bound in China
10 9 8 7 6 5 4 3 2 1

 Harry N. Abrams, Inc.
100 Fifth Avenue
New York, N.Y. 10011
www.abramsbooks.com

Abrams is a subsidiary of
 LA MARTINIÈRE
GROUPE